STINKBIRD HAS A SUPERPOWER

JILL ESBAUM   illustrated by BOB SHEA

putnam

G. P. PUTNAM'S SONS

For Lawson —J.E.
For Colleen and Ryan —B.S.

G. P. PUTNAM'S SONS
An imprint of Penguin Random House LLC, New York

First published in the United States of America by G. P. Putnam's Sons,
an imprint of Penguin Random House LLC, 2023

Visit us online at penguinrandomhouse.com.

Library of Congress Cataloging-in-Publication Data
Names: Esbaum, Jill, author. | Shea, Bob, illustrator.
Title: Stinkbird has a superpower / Jill Esbaum;
illustrated by Bob Shea.
Description: New York: G. P. Putnam's Sons, 2023. |
Summary: "A father hoatzin who lives near the Amazon
River can't help bragging about his chick's special
talents"—Provided by publisher.
Identifiers: LCCN 2022006914 (print) |
LCCN 2022006915 (ebook) | ISBN 9780593529522 (hardcover) |
ISBN 9780593529539 (epub) | ISBN 9780593529546 (kindle edition)
Subjects: LCSH: Hoactzin—Juvenile fiction. | CYAC: Hoatzins—Fiction. |
Birds—Fiction. | Animal defenses—Fiction. | Animals—Infancy—Fiction. |
Father and child—Fiction. | LCGFT: Animal fiction. | Picture books.
Classification: LCC PZ10.3.E7195 St 2023 (print) | LCC PZ10.3.E7195 (ebook) |
DDC [E]—dc23
LC record available at https://lccn.loc.gov/2022006914
LC ebook record available at https://lccn.loc.gov/2022006915

Manufactured in China

ISBN 9780593529522
10 9 8 7 6 5 4 3 2 1
TOPL

Design by Suki Boynton • Text set in Linotype Syntax Letter Com
The art was made with diligence, love, and Procreate.

HELLO, PEOPLE. I am a hoatzin.
You can say it—WHOT-sin.
Handsome, aren't I?

Like every other bird, I have wings.
Feathers. A beak. Like many other birds,
I live in the Amazon rain forest and
nowhere else on Earth.

Unlike any other bird, we hoatzins
have an amazing superpower that—

Here in the Amazon, many creatures eat other creatures to stay alive. But I am lucky. No creature wants to eat me. That's because—

You're SCARY!

Who, me?

You fly HIGH!

No. I am lucky
to reach the lowest
branches.

The thing that puts off predators and
gives me the nickname Stinkbird is . . .

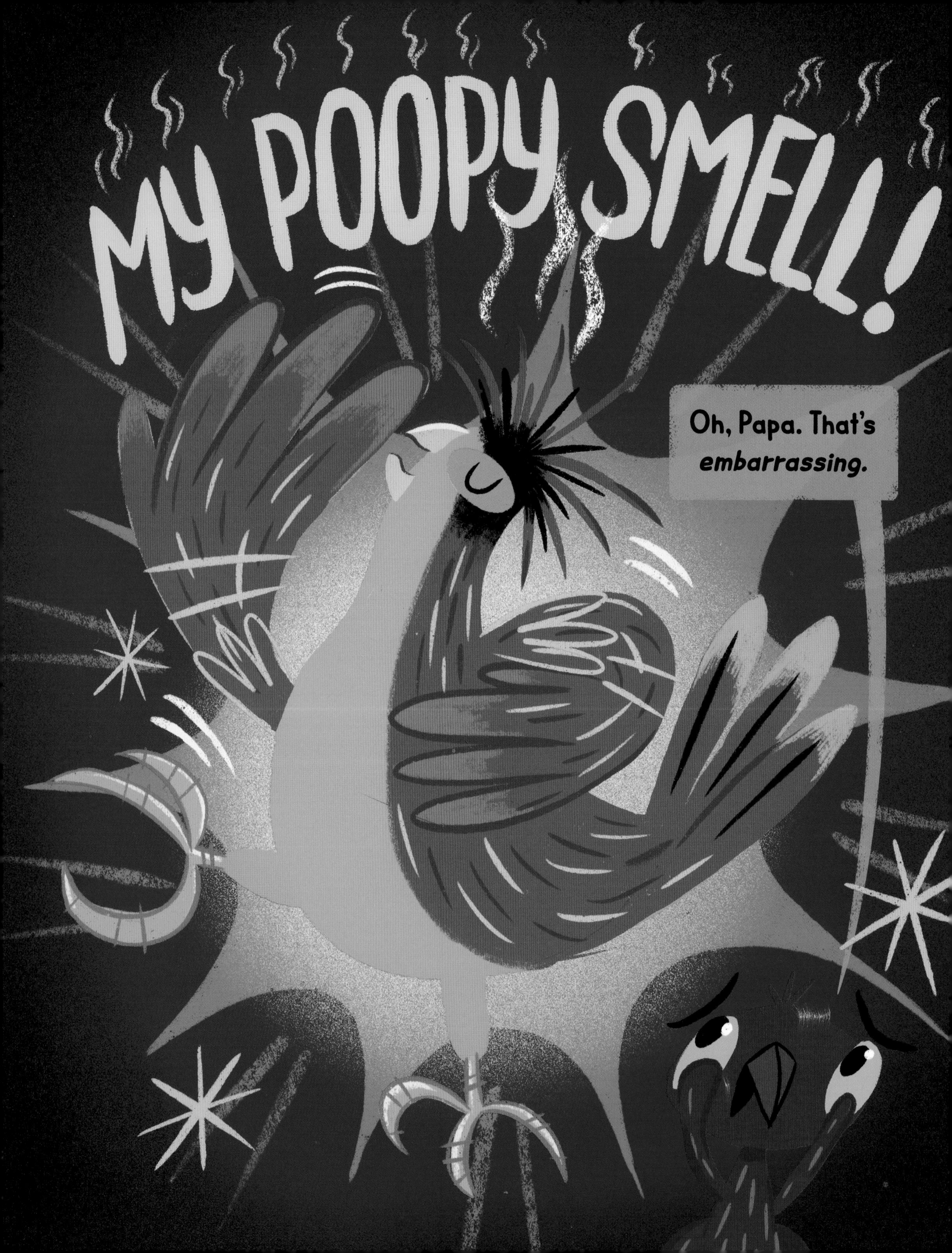
MY POOPY SMELL!
Oh, Papa. That's *embarrassing.*

My song is not the superpower either. But it is loud and beautiful. Especially when my flock and I sing together. Ready, friends? **GO!**

My mate and I find a low branch that sweeps out above a river. Then we pile a loose bundle of sticks like so, and ta-da! Does this seem like a perilous place for our chicks?

Ah. That's the clever part. Because while parents are away eating leaves, chicks are alone. Remember how no creatures bother stinky *adult* hoatzins? That is not true of our precious eggs and chicks. They are a favorite food of monkeys and snakes. Large birds too. Eagles. Falcons. Hawks.

Food?
I'm food?!

So what do our
smart chicks do when
danger nears?

Tell me! Tell me!
Tell me!

They fall into
the river.

Worry not, good people.
Hoatzin chicks can swim.

It's true. I'm not pulling your wing.
See him flap-flap-flapping underwater?
Go, chick, go!

At the riverbank, the chicks cling to a root
or stick until the predator goes away.

Did you see, Papa?
Did you see me *swimming*?
What a cool superpower!

That is not the
superpower, son.
Many birds can swim.

Oh.

Brace yourselves, people, for something astonishing.
After a chick falls into the river and swims to safety, it . . .

Do you see what makes a hoatzin chick different from every other chick in the world? Claws. On their *wings*. We are born with them. They give us our amazing superpower: *climbing*.

Do I have them? No. As we grow, the claws disappear. Only hoatzin chicks can climb like little acrobats.

I am so proud.

Proud of my
handsome self.

Proud to be a hoatzin. Or, if people want to use my nickname—

BURRRRRRP!

STINKBIRD!

"Phew. Stinky burp. You're getting there, son!!"

TRUE OR FALSE?

Hoatzins are the only birds that eat nothing but leaves.

TRUE. Different kinds of birds eat different kinds of things, like berries, bugs, bits of fruit, grains and grasses, seeds, and nuts. Some birds even eat leaves. But the hoatzin is the only bird that eats *nothing* but leaves. Hey, a bird likes what a bird likes!

Stinky adult hoatzins don't have to worry about predators.

TRUE. Hoatzins have a large pouch, before the stomach, where leaves are broken into little bits. Along the way, helpful bacteria (teeny-tiny critters that live in stomachs) turn the leaf bits into:

1. nutrients that help keep a bird healthy
2. waste (poop)

Because that process takes so long, the waste has plenty of time to get super stinky. The yucky smell of a whole flock of hoatzins is enough to make even the hungriest predator lose its appetite.

Hoatzins do not really burp.

FALSE. They do! As leaves break down and get juicy inside a bird's body, they create a gas called methane. That gas has to go somewhere—like out. *Buuurrrrp!*

Hoatzin chicks are the only birds born with wing claws.

TRUE. But millions of years ago, a small flying dinosaur called archaeopteryx also had claws on its wings. That causes many scientists to believe that the two creatures may be related.

Hoatzin chicks cannot fly during their first year of life.

FALSE. They learn to fly when they are about seventy days old (a little over two months).

A hoatzin chick is able to fall from its nest and swim underwater to escape danger.

TRUE. *Splish-splash!*

Hoatzins are proud of themselves.

FALSE (*probably*). Scientists believe some birds feel simple emotions, like joy, anger, affection, and sadness. But a complicated human emotion like pride? Not likely . . . which is too bad, because hoatzins have so much to be proud of. *Skrawk!*

Hoatzins can talk.

Hmm. What do YOU think?

NOTE: This manuscript was vetted by Thomas S. Schulenberg, research associate at Cornell Lab of Ornithology and co-author of *Birds of Peru*.

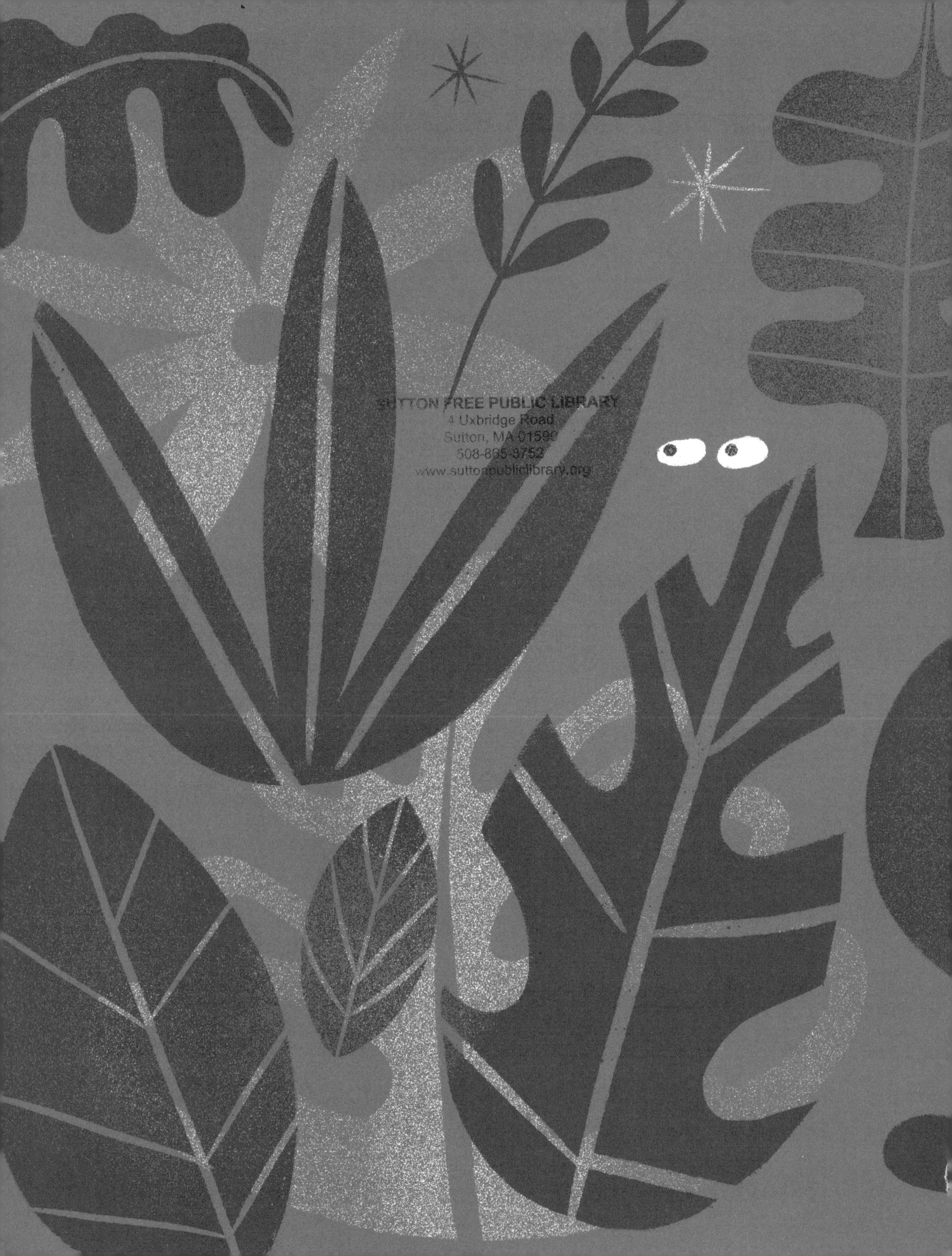